For G5 and Corbin, let
books be your multi-pass.
—A.L.

I Can Read Book® is a trademark of HarperCollins Publishers.

Chicken in Charge
Copyright © 2019 by HarperCollins Publishers
All rights reserved. Manufactured in China.
No part of this book may be used or reproduced in any manner whatsoever without written permission except
in the case of brief quotations embodied in critical articles and reviews. For information address HarperCollins
Children's Books, a division of HarperCollins Publishers, 195 Broadway, New York, NY 10007.
www.icanread.com

Library of Congress Control Number: 2018942093
ISBN 978-0-06-236425-8 (trade bdg.)—ISBN 978-0-06-236424-1 (pbk.)

Book design by Celeste Knudsen

18 19 20 21 22 SCP 10 9 8 7 6 5 4 3 2 1

First Edition

I Can Read!™

BEGINNING 1 READING

CHICKEN in CHARGE

By Adam Lehrhaupt
Pictures by Shahar Kober

HARPER
An Imprint of HarperCollinsPublishers

"The farmer is away," said Sam.

"Who is caring for the new lambs?"

"I am!" said Zoey.

"This chicken is in charge!"

"Is that a good plan?" asked Sam.

"What do you know about lambs?"

"I know all about lambs," said Zoey.

"They need dinner and baths.

After that, we put them to bed."

"That sounds easy," said Sam.

"Where do we start?"

Zoey headed off to the barn.

"Dinner," she said.

"That's my favorite meal," said Sam.

He hurried to catch up to Zoey.

Zoey grabbed a pie for the lambs.

"Do lambs like pie?" asked Sam.

"I thought they ate grass."

"Don't be silly," said Zoey.

"Everyone likes pie."

"Good point," said Sam.

"Good job eating!" said Zoey.

Sam looked at the lambs.

They were covered in pie.

"I think it's bath time," said Sam.

13

Zoey hauled out a tub of water.

"Is the tub big enough?" asked Sam.

"We're not using this," said Zoey.

She dumped out the water.

A muddy puddle formed at Sam's feet.

"We're taking mud baths," Zoey said.

"It's the best way to get clean."

"Everyone in!" said Zoey.

"Time for your baths."

The lambs piled into the mud pit.

So did Sam.

Even Zoey joined the fun.

CANNONBALL!

"That was great," said Sam.

He shook off the mud.

The lambs tried to shake off, too.

They were not successful.

"They don't look clean," said Sam.

"Of course not," said Zoey.

"There's one more step for lambs."

"What's the step?" asked Sam.

"They need to dry off," said Zoey.

"Everyone into the hay!"

The lambs tumbled in.

"They're covered in hay," said Sam.

"And completely dry," said Zoey.

"Time for bed."

"Where do lambs sleep?" asked Sam.

"In a nest," said Zoey.

"Come on . . . I'll show you."

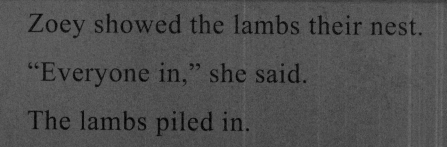

Zoey showed the lambs their nest.

"Everyone in," she said.

The lambs piled in.

They did not look ready to sleep.

"Settle down," said Zoey.

"I'll tell you a bedtime story."

When the lambs settled down,

Zoey told them a story.

It was a story about two friends.

It had asteroids.

It had comets.

It had alien spaceships.

The lambs did not fall asleep.

CHICKEN
in
SPACE

Zoey told another story.

This one was all about school.

CLARA
PIP
HENRY
SAM

CHICKEN IN SCHOOL

By Adam Lehrhaupt
Illustrated by Shahar Kober

It had books.

It had crayons.

It even had recess.

The lambs did not fall asleep.

Then Zoey told a tale of adventure.
It had a wild yeti.

It had a haunted barn.

It had pie.

When Zoey finished her story,
something amazing happened.
Everyone fell asleep.
Even Sam.